Spiky

Written and illustrated by Ilaria Guarducci

Translated by Laura Watkinson

amazon crossing **kids**

Previously published as *Spino* by Camelozampa in Italy in 2016. Translated from Italian by Laura Watkinson.
First published in English by Amazon Crossing Kids in collaboration with Amazon Crossing in 2019.

Published by Amazon Crossing Kids, New York, in collaboration with Amazon Crossing

www.apub.com

Amazon, Amazon Crossing, and all related logos are trademarks of Amazon.com, Inc., or its affiliates.

ISBN-13: 9781542040433 (hardcover)
ISBN-10: 1542040434 (hardcover)

The illustrations are rendered digitally.

Book design by Tanya Ross-Hughes
Printed in China

First Edition

10 9 8 7 6 5 4 3 2 1

In a dark, dark forest, there lived a creature who was covered in spikes.

His name was **Spiky**.

He had spikes on his back, spikes on his tummy, spikes on his head, and spikes on his bottom. He even had a few little spikes on his arms and his knees.

Spiky was very proud of his spikes. They were handy for chasing off robbers, they scared away anyone who was bigger than him, and they kept absolutely everyone at a distance.

He was spiky,
he was bad,
and he didn't need
anyone at all.

His father, Mr. Spikington, had sent him to the best school
for badness in the whole country.

Spiky had learned all the latest scare techniques, the snarkiest snarl,
and a wide variety of terrifying expressions.

But most important of all,
he had learned that he was
very, very bad indeed.

And since Spiky had been living all alone in the dark, dark forest, he had become even more wicked.

He sharpened his spikes to make the points perfect.
Then he went out into the dark, dark wood, raising a ruckus,
stealing snacks, and tormenting the trees.

He pulled the wings off butterflies.
If he couldn't fly, why should they?

He captured the robins and the chickadees in big glass jars
because their chirping annoyed him so much.

What was there to be happy about?

He plucked the petals off the flowers,
he pricked holes in the snails' shells
because they were slow and slimy,
and he laughed at the toads for being so ugly.

Spiky had become so **very, very bad**
that even his shadow grew darker and darker.

But one day something unexpected happened.
Spiky started losing his spikes.

The **first** spike suddenly dropped out onto the floor of the dining room.

The **second**, soon after that, in the living room.
A few minutes later, the **third** one fell,

and the **fourth,**   and the **fifth** . . .   and, after a while,
he lost count.

Before long, all the dark spikes were gone,
and Spiky was as **soft** and as **pink**
as a soft, pink **marshmallow**.

Noooooooooi

He didn't scare anyone now.

The snails sneered, and the toads tittered.

The butterflies landed on his soft, pink bottom,
mistaking it for a rosebud.

Without his spikes, Spiky was **harmless**.
And a little bit silly.
He felt completely lost.
With no spikes, his life was pointless.
Whatever would he do with his days?

Spiky spent his time sitting on the hardest rock in the forest,
feeling very sad and sorry for himself.

One afternoon, Bernardo the bunny came hopping along.
"Hey there!" he said. "What's wrong?"

"I'm sad," replied Spiky. "Without my spikes,
I don't feel like Spiky anymore. I don't know what to do."

"I see," said Bernardo, who was a very wise little bunny. "Come with me."

Spiky went. He had nothing better to do.

They went for a long walk through the forest. Bernardo took him
to amazing spots with beautiful views of the whole valley.

They chatted about serious things . . .

and about less serious things.

In the days that followed, Bernardo invited Spiky to his burrow
near the lake so he could get to know the rest of the family.

They went for long, cool swims and had diving competitions.

Spiky felt the breeze on his soft skin.
He could sunbathe and roll about in the meadow,
with the blades of grass tickling his pink back.

SOLAR BRONZE

He saw that there were
so many things he could still do,
even without spikes.
He could play ball
(and it didn't burst!).

He could be close to others.

Very close.

Very, very close.

Closer than he'd ever been before.

And it was
a good feeling.

By now he was getting used to his pink skin. But one morning he woke up
with a strange itch . . . He looked at himself in the mirror and saw
that lots and lots of little spikes were growing again—all over his back, his tummy,
his head, and his bottom. Perhaps being soft and pink was just a phase . . .

"**Aha!**" he thought at first. "**Spiky the Spiteful is back!**"

Spiky had been born to scare everyone and to play nasty tricks.
Maybe it was time to return to his old way of life.

Spiky decided to give it a try. So he ran out to raise a ruckus.

As he went by, the toads hopped into the pond, the snails ran away as fast as
their slime could carry them, and the chickadees flew for shelter
among the leaves of the trees.

Everything seemed to have gone back to the way it was before.

But for Spiky, it didn't feel the same.
All that scariness . . . what was the point?

He went back to his usual rock to contemplate.

And, when he thought about it, those big old trees sheltered him
from the summer sun with their leafy branches,
the butterflies and the flowers gave the forest a nice touch of color,
the chickadees weren't that annoying,
and the snails . . .
hmm, no, the snails really were revolting.

"What's wrong?"
Bernardo asked him again.

"I'm confused," said Spiky.
"You know, my spikes
have grown back."

"I can see that."

"Don't I scare you?"

"No, you're still you,
with or without spikes," said Bernardo,
who was indeed a very wise little bunny.
"**Come on**! The others are waiting
for us at the lake!"

And so they spent another afternoon together . . .

. . . and then another . . .

and another...

and yet another...

And it was
a very, very good feeling.